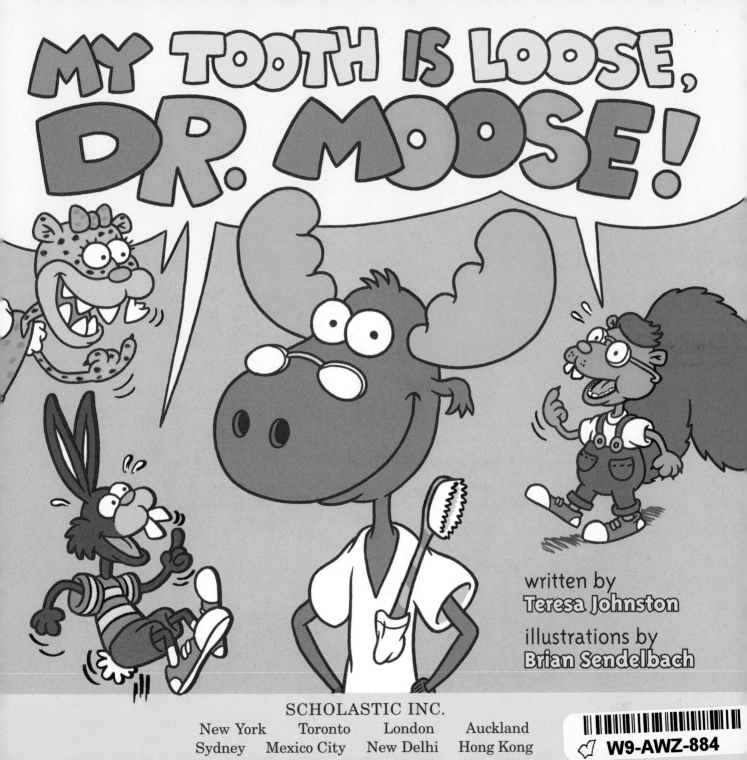

To my mom, who has always supported me, in whatever direction
I have decided to take with my life

—T.J.

For Albin and Rose

—B.S.

Library of Congress Cataloging-in-Publication Data is available.

ISBN 978-0-545-28910-8

10 9 8 7 6 5 4 3   13 14 15 16

Printed in the U.S.A.   40
First printing, January 2012
Book design by Becky James

Dr. Moose is the town dentist.

Dr. Moose can clean teeth. Dr. Moose can check for cavities.
But Dr. Moose's favorite thing to help with is a loose tooth.

Carla Crocodile works with Dr. Moose. She looks at the schedule and exclaims, "What a busy day!"

10 A.M. LILY LEOPARD

11 A.M. SIMON SQUIRREL

2 P.M. HARRIET HIPPO

4 P.M. BENJAMIN BUNNY

She pushes the intercom button. "Ready, Dr. Moose?" she asks.
"It's time to smile, Carla Crocodile!" the dentist replies.

"Lily Leopard," Carla Crocodile says. "Dr. Moose will see you now."
Lily jumps up and follows Carla Crocodile into Dr. Moose's office.

Lily Leopard leaps into the dentist's chair.

"What seems to be the problem?" asks Dr. Moose.

Lily Leopard points to her front tooth and says, "My tooth is loose, Dr. Moose!"

"What fun!" Dr. Moose replies. "Start wiggling it. I'll be right back!"

When Dr. Moose returns, Lily Leopard is holding her tooth in her paw. "The wiggling worked," she shouts.

"Moose Magic!" he says.

Simon Squirrel is running late. His tooth is loose, which makes it hard for him to gather nuts.

He finally makes it to Dr. Moose's office.

"Ready, Dr. Moose?" Carla Crocodile calls over the intercom.

"Simon Squirrel, Dr. Moose will see you now," she says.

Simon Squirrel scurries into the dentist's chair.

"My tooth is loose, Dr. Moose!" Simon Squirrel says. "Only problem is, I don't know what to do. My sister says to push my tooth. My brother says to pull it. I'm too scared to do it."

"Don't worry, Simon Squirrel. We'll get this all sorted out," Dr. Moose says.

"Why don't we work together to help you with your tooth? You can push, and I will pull."

A second later, Simon Squirrel's tooth pops right out!

"It worked! How did you know it would work?" asks Simon Squirrel.

Dr. Moose chuckles and says, "Sometimes all it takes is a little Moose Magic."

"Good luck collecting nuts," Dr. Moose says. "Your new tooth will grow in before you know it."

Carla Crocodile looks at the clock. She presses the intercom button. "Next appointment, Dr. Moose?" she asks.

Carla Crocodile checks the schedule. "Harriet Hippo," she calls. "It's time for your cleaning."

Carla Crocodile shows Harriet Hippo into the dentist's office. Harriet sits down in the dentist's chair.

Harriet Hippo loves going to Dr. Moose and getting her teeth cleaned. She opens her mouth wide.

"You don't have any cavities," Dr. Moose says, looking inside her very big mouth. "Now let's get those teeth cleaned!"

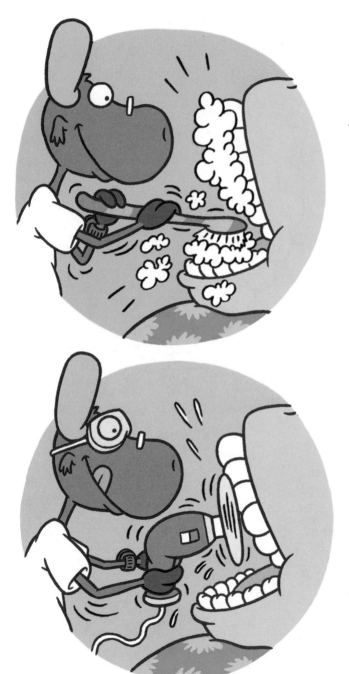

Dr. Moose brushes Harriet Hippo's teeth. He flosses between her teeth.

Then he uses a big electric sander to polish her teeth.

"All done," Dr. Moose says, smiling.

"Oh, Dr. Moose!" Harriet Hippo exclaims. "My teeth are so clean they shine! You do wonderful work!"

"Now remember to keep them clean at home," says Dr. Moose.

"I will, Dr. Moose. Thank you!" Harriet Hippo climbs off the chair.

Benjamin Bunny has the last appointment of the day. He is going to see Dr. Moose because he has a loose tooth.

Benjamin Bunny cannot sit still. He jumps from chair to chair.

Carla Crocodile presses the button on the intercom.
"Ready, Dr. Moose?" Carla Crocodile calls.

"Benjamin Bunny," she says. "Dr. Moose will see you now."

Benjamin Bunny gets up and hops into the dentist's office. He jumps into the chair. His tail twitches.

"What can I help you with, Benjamin Bunny?" Dr. Moose asks.

"My tooth is loose, Dr. Moose," Benjamin tells him. "And it's almost carrot season!"

"I can help with that," Dr. Moose says. "How about you take a bite of this big crunchy carrot so that we can get an idea of how loose that tooth is?"

As soon as Benjamin Bunny bites into the carrot, his tooth falls out of his mouth.

"All it took was some Moose Magic," says Dr. Moose.

Benjamin Bunny decides that going to the dentist is nothing to be nervous about.

When you have a loose tooth, go see Dr. Moose!